WHIZ BANG, ZOOM!

WHIZ BANG, ZOOM!

Ethan Flask and Professor von Offel's
Energetic Experiments

MAD SCIENCE

by Kathy Burkett

SCHOLASTIC INC.

New York   Toronto   London   Auckland   Sydney
Mexico City   New Delhi   Hong Kong

Table of Contents

Prologue

For more than 100 years, the Flasks, the town of Arcana's first family of science, have been methodically, precisely, safely, *scientifically* inventing all kinds of things.

For more than 100 years, the von Offels, Arcana's first family of sneaks, have been stealing those inventions.

Where the Flasks are brilliant, rational, and reliable, the von Offels are brilliant, reckless, and ruthless. The nearly fabulous Flasks could have earned themselves a major chapter in the history of science — but at every key moment, there always seemed to be a von Offel on the scene to "borrow" a science notebook, beat a Flask to the punch on a patent, or booby-trap an important experiment. Just take a look at the Flask family tree and then the von Offel clan. Coincidence? Or *evidence*!

Despite being tricked out of fame and fortune by the awful von Offels, the Flasks doggedly continued their scientific inquiries. The last of the family line, Ethan Flask, is no exception. An outstanding sixth-grade science teacher, he's also conducting studies into animal intelligence and is competing for the Third Millennium Foundation's prestigious Vanguard Teacher Award. Unfortunately, the person who's evaluating Ethan for the award is none other than Professor John von Offel, a.k.a. the original mad scientist, Johannes von Offel.

In *What's the Big Idea? Ethan Flask and Professor von Offel's Ingenious Inventions*, the professor's deanimator experiment went haywire — and he reanimated two long-lost von Offels. Now the professor has his hands full trying to keep Esmerelda von Offel Loch and Éduard von Offel in line. After all, they may interfere with his high-flying plans to hijack Mr. Flask's catapult.

You'll find step-by-step instructions for the experiment mentioned on page 36 of this book in *Energy Science,* the Mad Science Experiments Log.

The Nearly Fabulous Flasks

Jedidiah Flask
2nd person to create rubber band

Oliver Flask
Missed appointment to patent new glue because he was mysteriously epoxied to his chair

Augustus Flask
Developed telephone; got a busy signal

Mildred Flask Tachyon
Tranquilizer formula never registered; carriage horses fell asleep en route to patent office

Percy Flask
Lost notes on cure for common cold in pickpocketing incident

Lane Tachyon
Developed laughing gas; was kept in hysterics while a burglar stole the formula

Archibald Flask
Knocked out cold en route to patent superior baseball bat

Marlow Flask
Runner-up to Adolphus von Offel for Sir Isaac Newton Science Prize

Amaryllis Flask Lepton
Discovered new kind of amoeba; never published findings due to dysentery

Norton Flask
Clubbed with an overcooked
meat loaf and robbed of prototype
microwave oven

Salome Flask Rhombus
Discovered cloud-salting with dry
ice; never made it to patent office
due to freak downpour

Roland Flask
His new high-speed engine was
believed to have powered the getaway car
that stole his prototype

Constance Rhombus Ampère
Lost Marie Curie award to
Beatrice O'Door; voted
Miss Congeniality

Margaret Flask Geiger
Name was mysteriously
deleted from registration
papers for her undetectable
correction fluid

Michael Flask
Arrived with gas grill
schematic only to find
tailgate party outside
patent office

Solomon Ampère
Bionic horse placed in
Kentucky Derby after
von Offel entry

Ethan Flask

The Awful von Offels

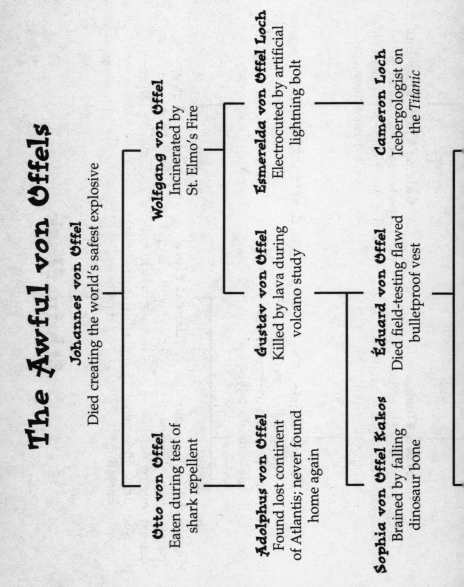

Johannes von Offel
Died creating the world's safest explosive

Wolfgang von Offel
Incinerated by
St. Elmo's Fire

Esmerelda von Offel Loch
Electrocuted by artificial
lightning bolt

Cameron Loch
Icebergologist on
the *Titanic*

Otto von Offel
Eaten during test of
shark repellent

Gustav von Offel
Killed by lava during
volcano study

Éduard von Offel
Died field-testing flawed
bulletproof vest

Adolphus von Offel
Found lost continent
of Atlantis; never found
home again

Sophia von Offel Kakos
Brained by falling
dinosaur bone

Rula von Offel Malle
Evaporated

Kurt von Offel
Weak batteries in antigravity backpack

Beatrice Malle O'Door
Drowned pursuing the Loch Ness Monster

Colin von Offel
Transplanted his brain into wildebeest

Feldspar O'Door
Died of freezer burn during cryogenics experiment

Alan von Offel
Failed to survive field test of nonpoisonous arsenic

Felicity von Offel Day
Brained by diving bell during deep-sea exploration

Professor John von Offel (?)

Johannes von Offel's
Book of Scientific Observations,
1891

In a show of youthful vigor and mischief, my grandchildren built a large catapult and began lobbing rotten fruit at the Flask house. There I was, basking in the glow of my descendants' roguish brilliance, when who should emerge from the besieged mansion but Jedidiah Flask himself. He launched into a speech predictably rife with moral platitudes. Meanwhile Esmerelda, the youngest, loaded the catapult with a watermelon of remarkable size. Her aim was true, and Jedidiah was forced to retreat.

I believe I can safely report that the von Offel spirit is alive in the younger generation.

CHAPTER 1

Gag Lunch

Prescott Forrester lowered his lunch tray to the table as if it were piled with nuclear waste.

Alberta Wong stirred her pool of gray-green peas with a plastic spoon. "I've got to start bringing lunch," she said. "At least until Dr. Kepler hires a new cafeteria cook."

Prescott nodded miserably. "My mom usually packs me a bag lunch." He prodded a soggy fish stick with his fork. "She *would* pick this week to go on a business trip. My dad always just gives me money to buy lunch."

"Your mom had no way of knowing Mr. Klumpp would be filling in as cook." Alberta leaned closer to her tray. "I think he must have sterilized these peas instead of steaming them."

Luis Antilla slid in beside Alberta and dumped out his bag lunch. Prescott and Alberta stared as their friend unwrapped a peanut butter and jelly sandwich and opened a bag of pretzels. Prescott felt himself salivating.

1

Luis didn't even look up. "Oh, all right," he said, pushing the pretzels toward Prescott and Alberta. "But tomorrow, it's every kid for himself or herself. It's not that hard to open a jar of peanut butter and make your own sandwich."

Prescott popped a pretzel into his mouth. "I know, I know," he said. "But I think packing my lunch makes my mom feel useful."

Alberta rolled her eyes. "Like your mom's that pitiful."

Prescott shoved his tray aside and reached for another pretzel. "I can't even believe Dr. Kepler is letting Mr. Klumpp serve this stuff. I hate to waste food, but this isn't fit for human consumption." He glanced back at the tray. "Actually, I wouldn't feed it to an animal, either."

Alberta laughed. "Maybe we could take it back to the lab and perform a science experiment on it."

Sean Baxter dropped his tray on the table and slid in beside Prescott. "I'm sure there's a law against having hazardous materials in the classroom."

Luis glanced across the cafeteria and made a face. "Don't look now, but Professor von Offel is going back for seconds. If that stuff is as deadly as it looks, he'll be a ghost again before science class starts."

"He did manage to survive eating dog food and sawdust modeling dough," Alberta said. "But those peas might just finish him off."

Across the room, Mr. Flask stood motionless on the cafeteria line. His eyes shifted from one steaming bin of gray-and-beige food to the next. The professor stood behind him, with Atom on his shoulder.

Mr. Klumpp crossed his arms. "Let's move this along, Flask. I have *appreciative* customers waiting." He nodded his head toward the professor.

The teacher swallowed. "I'd like, uh — well, what would you suggest?"

"It's all equally good," the custodian said.

"I bet," Mr. Flask muttered. He bit his lower lip. "Well, how about some of those mashed potatoes?"

"That's whipped cauliflower." Mr. Klumpp spooned a large dollop onto Mr. Flask's plate.

"And gravy?" the teacher said.

"Cheese sauce," Mr. Klumpp corrected him.

"Those mini meatballs look interesting."

The custodian scooped out a large spoonful. "These are peas."

"Oh." Mr. Flask smiled weakly and reached for his tray. "Well, that's a start."

"*There's* Professor von Offel!" said a voice behind them.

The professor turned and froze. Dr. Kepler strode across the cafeteria, leading the professor's two newly reanimated descendants, his granddaughter, Esmerelda von Offel Loch, and her nephew, Éduard von Offel. Both were dressed in traditional clothing not much more modern than the professor's own.

"I've brought your — colleagues?" The principal looked to the professor for confirmation.

He stared at her blankly.

3

Dr. Kepler turned back to Éduard and his Aunt Esmerelda. "And what a coincidence," she said. "Here's Ethan Flask, the teacher Professor von Offel is evaluating for the Vanguard Teacher Award." She looked at them curiously. "I assume you are interested in meeting him?"

Aunt Esmerelda strode forward and offered Mr. Flask her hand. "Oh, we've met already," she said. "But we *are* very interested in him."

The teacher smiled uncertainly and shook her hand.

"You've met?" Dr. Kepler asked Mr. Flask.

"They were at the state capitol building during our field trip," the teacher said.

Dr. Kepler nodded. "I suppose the Millennium Foundation would have its regional headquarters in the state capitol." Her eyes flicked down to Mr. Flask's brown-and-beige lunch. "Oh," she said flatly. "I *was* going to suggest that we all sit down and eat together, but —"

"Out of the question," Éduard said.

"Nonsense!" Aunt Esmerelda said. "It's a marvelous idea!" She picked up a tray and handed it to Éduard.

"We really shouldn't," he said.

"Don't be rude, darling," she said, handing him a tray.

Aunt Esmerelda picked up a tray of her own and headed to the cafeteria line. "I'll have some of everything," she told Mr. Klumpp.

The custodian's face brightened. "Another enthu-siastic customer."

"I know a lady should eat like a bird," Aunt Es-merelda said as Mr. Klumpp filled her tray. "How-ever, I have a predisposition for thinking big. I know not everyone agrees, but I think there's a glory in taking things to extremes, don't you?"

"Absolutely!" the custodian said. "Anything worth doing is worth doing well. My personal passion is keeping this school building clean." He looked down at the colorless food and blushed slightly. "Cooking is not even really a sideline for me." He handed Aunt Esmerelda her lunch, then reached for Éduard's tray. "What can I get for you?"

Éduard pointed at a serving pan.

Mr. Klumpp thrust his scoop into the whipped cauliflower.

"I was always partial to gruel," Éduard said.

Aunt Esmerelda carried her tray to the lunch table where Mr. Flask sat talking to Dr. Kepler. Professor von Offel slumped at the other end, silently eating his food. When Aunt Esmerelda inserted herself between the teacher and the professor, von Offel grumbled. A moment later, Éduard sat down opposite them.

"I hope the two of you will be able to stay and observe Mr. Flask's sixth-grade science class," Dr. Kepler said.

Éduard cleared his throat. "I believe I speak for us both when I say that would be terribly improper," he said.

"What would be improper would be for us to refuse such a gracious invitation!" Aunt Esmerelda smiled and leaned toward Mr. Flask. "We'd love to observe your star teacher."

Mr. Flask smiled uncomfortably.

"How long will you be in Arcana?" the principal asked.

"We're leaving as soon as possible." Éduard turned toward the professor. "As soon as *someone* can work out the details."

"Has your car broken down?" the principal said. "I could get a mechanic to look at it during sixth-grade science."

"Oh, it's nothing like that," Aunt Esmerelda said. "Please don't give it another thought. We could be here days or even weeks. We'll just use that extra time in Arcana to observe your Mr. Flask."

Dr. Kepler looked startled. "Weeks? But I thought the professor's Vanguard Teacher Award observation report was due this Friday." She looked at the professor, who stared back vacantly. Then she turned to the other two von Offels. "Well, of course, you should take as much time as you need." She forced a smile. "I only hope our cafeteria food doesn't scare you away."

"Oh, it just needs a little spice," Aunt Esmerelda said. She stood up and gestured toward the kitchen. "May I?"

"Of course," the principal replied. Aunt Esmerelda excused herself with a slight curtsy. Dr. Kepler looked around the table. The professor was shooing Atom away from his tray. Éduard was staring at the bank of fluorescent lights above him. Dr. Kepler leaned toward Mr. Flask and whispered, "I realize it's inconvenient to have two more visitors in your classroom. But I can't help suspecting that the professor is, well, not completely on the ball. When I asked about his observation report, he didn't even look that interested. Maybe having his colleagues here will give you a fairer chance of winning the award."

The teacher nodded.

"Here we go!" said a cheerful voice behind them. Aunt Esmerelda pushed Mr. Flask's tray to one side. In its place, she set a plate heaped with whipped cauliflower. "What do you think?"

The teacher scooped up a spoonful and put it into his mouth. Almost immediately, his face turned red. He grabbed his glass of water and started gulping it desperately.

"Oh, dear," Aunt Esmerelda said. "I must have put too much spice in. It's just that I normally like to work on a bigger scale." She took one spoonful of the spicy cauliflower and mixed it with Mr. Flask's original serving. "Try it now," she suggested.

The teacher winced, but he reached for a second bite. After a moment, he smiled. "Hey, that's really good!" Then his eyes grew wide and he dropped his spoon.

CHAPTER 2

Chaos Theory

"Is something else wrong?" Aunt Esmerelda asked.

"Not with the food," the teacher answered, standing up. He rushed to a corner of the cafeteria, where the air was thick with flying peas.

"It's the cops!" yelled Sean Baxter. "Everyone drop your weapons!" He made a big show of letting his spoon fall to the table.

Mr. Klumpp also stomped over to the table, his face red with anger. "I should have known it would be your sixth graders," he said to Mr. Flask. "I demand that these students serve detention for this outrage — three weeks minimum!"

Mr. Flask looked from Alberta to Luis to Prescott and shook his head. "I'm almost inclined to agree," he said. "I support your right to goof around a little at lunch, but you were just making a big mess."

"We're sorry, Mr. Flask," Alberta began. "We —"

"Hey, you don't mind a mess in class," Sean said.

Mr. Klumpp frowned at the teacher. "That's what

I was going to say. Your classroom methods promote this kind of thing!"

"Science *can* be messy," Mr. Flask said. "But it's mess with a purpose." He pointed to the scattered peas on the floor, some of which had already been stepped on. "This is a pointless mess."

"No, this was science, too," Sean said.

Mr. Flask crossed his arms. "What science — chaos theory?"

"Watch!" Sean loaded a spoon with peas and pulled it back with one finger. "Potential energy" — he lifted his finger, and the peas shot out of the spoon and splattered against the wall — "and kinetic energy."

The teacher suppressed a smile. "True —"

"What?" the custodian cried.

"Well, technically, he's right," Mr. Flask said. He turned back to the sixth graders. "And since you've shown an interest in the topic, this seems like a perfect time to start a unit on energy." He smiled wryly. "But from now on, we'll keep our 'energetic' studies out of the cafeteria, right?"

"And who will clean up this mess?" Mr. Klumpp demanded, waving a rag in the air.

"They will," the teacher replied. He took the rag from Mr. Klumpp and handed it to Sean. "And I guarantee they'll leave it spotless."

About an hour later, the professor was reluctantly leading his descendants toward the science lab.

"It's bad enough that you've crowded into the von Offel mansion," he complained.

"It's never been more livable!" Atom said. "With Esmerelda cooking and patching the holes in the ceiling and —"

"Thank you, dear," Aunt Esmerelda said.

The professor frowned. "Well, you have no right to be *here*, in this school, never mind passing yourselves off as representatives of the Third Millennium Foundation."

"Well, after all, *you* were the one who brought us back to life, you and your silly reanimator. And as to our identities, we had to make up *something* to satisfy the very curious Dr. Kepler," Éduard said with a sniff. "Really, sir. This is all very inappropriate. You went to the grave more than a hundred years ago, and that's where you should return."

"But I have a legitimate reason for being here," the professor said. "As the principal mentioned, I'm —" He thought for a moment.

"Evaluating Mr. Flask for the Vanguard Teacher Award," Atom provided.

"Oh, not that frivolous nonsense," the professor said.

Atom raised a feathered eyebrow. "Oh, you meant your own personal agenda?"

"Of course," the professor replied. "What could be more important?"

"Well, I think it's lovely that you're in a position to

help that charming Ethan Flask," Aunt Esmerelda said.

"Who said anything about helping him?" the professor snapped. "Von Offels don't help Flasks. Flasks help von Offels — unwittingly, of course."

"Well, I think it's time we put all of that behind us," Aunt Esmerelda said.

Éduard nodded. "It's only fair. Remember, the von Offels died out years ago." He looked pointedly at the professor. "That's the way it was meant to be."

"I'm rather enjoying my second chance at life," Aunt Esmerelda said. "But it is a new era, at any rate. You know, Ethan Flask reminds me a bit of Jedidiah." She giggled. "Though I bet he'd be better at ducking a flying watermelon."

"A flying watermelon?" Éduard asked, scowling.

Aunt Esmerelda smiled. "I guess your father never told you about that."

They came to a stop in front of the science lab door.

"Oh, there's that darling man now," Aunt Esmerelda said. She smoothed down her skirts and sailed through the door, with Éduard and the professor trailing behind.

CHAPTER 3

The Work of the Cosmos

"Welcome to sixth-grade science," Mr. Flask told Aunt Esmerelda and Éduard.

Éduard walked over to a tripod that stood at the front of class. "What is *this*?" he demanded.

"Some people are surprised to see video cameras in science classrooms," Mr. Flask said. "But they're really great observation tools. You'll see one in action today."

Éduard traced the path of a cable that ran out of the back of the camera across Mr. Flask's desk and attached to — "And what is this?" he asked.

The teacher smiled. "Not exactly standard issue, is it? To get the speed I need for video, I've had to cobble together a few different systems."

"Hmmm." Éduard scowled down at the keyboard. "Clearly, this is a newfangled typewriter." He pointed to one side. "But what is this?"

"You mean the mouse?" Mr. Flask asked, puzzled.

Éduard made a face. "You've even mechanized your vermin? How absurd!"

"Perhaps we should let the class get started," Aunt Esmerelda said. She smiled at the teacher. "I do hope you'll give us seats with a good view."

Mr. Flask reddened. "Well, we're going to be doing some 'energetic' experiments up here today, so I've set out some extra chairs for you near the professor's desk." He gestured toward the back of the class.

Aunt Esmerelda sighed theatrically. "I suppose that will have to do. But who will escort me to my seat?"

"I will," Éduard said gruffly. He held out his arm. Aunt Esmerelda smiled at Mr. Flask and shrugged.

Mr. Flask waited until they were seated. "Earlier today, Sean gave a science demonstration that I'd like him to repeat for the class — and for the video camera." He handed Sean a plastic spoon and a mini marshmallow. "Sorry, no peas," he said.

Sean walked to the front of the class. "Are you getting my best side?" he asked the teacher.

Mr. Flask gave him a thumbs-up from behind the video camera. "Please aim at the wall," he added.

"You're no fun!" Sean said.

In the back of the classroom, Éduard cleared his throat loudly. "In my day, children were seen and not heard," he said indignantly.

Mr. Flask motioned for Sean to continue.

Sean balanced the mini marshmallow on the spoon and pulled the spoon back with his finger. "I just said, 'potential energy'" — he lifted his finger and the marshmallow went flying — "and 'kinetic energy.'" The mini marshmallow bounced off the wall and rolled to a stop on the floor.

Mr. Flask stopped the video camera. "What did Sean mean by 'potential energy'?"

Alberta raised her hand. "It's a kind of hidden, or stored, energy that can be put to use later."

Prescott nodded. "I remember when you asked me to give a ball potential energy, and all you meant was that you wanted me to pick it up."

Mr. Flask smiled. "That's right. And how did you turn that potential energy into kinetic energy, or energy in motion?"

"By letting go," Prescott said. "The ball immediately fell, which is one kind of motion."

Mr. Flask nodded. "And with Sean's spoon, the kinetic energy made the spoon spring forward and the marshmallow fly through the air." He walked over to the computer and clicked through a few screens. "I'm going to replay Sean's action in slow motion. But first, I'm going to let you in on one of the secrets of the universe. Under normal circumstances, energy can be neither created nor destroyed. It can only be converted from one form to another." He hit a button on the computer, and the scene advanced in slow motion. "Okay, Sean is bending the spoon back. Put another way, he's doing work to store potential energy in the spoon." He pointed to the screen. "The energy is actually stored where the spoon is bent. When the spoon 'unbends,' that energy will become kinetic. The spoon will transfer some of its kinetic energy to the marshmallow and send it flying. He's about to let go — there." Mr. Flask froze the image with the mini marshmallow about a foot from the spoon.

Alberta raised her hand. "But if energy can't be created, where did that potential energy come from? Was it in Sean's body or something?"

"Great question!" Mr. Flask said. "In a way it was, but it was a different kind of potential energy. Both the potential and the kinetic energy we just saw were kinds of mechanical energy. When Sean's finger moved, that was kinetic mechanical energy again. But where did that energy come from?"

Heather Patterson wrinkled her nose. "Knowing Sean, junk food."

Mr. Flask laughed. "You're skipping a few steps, but essentially, the energy did come from food. It was stored in the body as chemical potential energy."

"Cool!" Sean said. "See, junk food is an important source of energy."

"Any food is a source of chemical potential energy," Mr. Flask said. "Let's say this energy came from the healthiest thing you ate today. What would that be?"

Sean thought for a moment. "I think I drank some orange juice with my sugar-frosted, cocoa-coated —"

Mr. Flask put up a hand. "Orange juice is a great example," he said. "So there's Sean's chemical potential energy. But where did *that* energy come from?"

Alberta raised her hand. "Well, oranges and orange trees." She thought for a moment. "Did it come from the Sun?"

The teacher nodded. "Light is a form of energy. And as you know, plants use sunlight to make their own food. Essentially, they take the light and convert it into chemical potential energy. Plants use that energy to grow and to make seeds. And a lot of times, a living thing, like Sean, comes along and swallows some of that chemical potential energy for itself."

Luis thought for a moment. "But the Sun has been sending out light for billions of years. So where does all that energy come from?"

"Well, I mentioned earlier that energy can't be created under ordinary conditions," the teacher said. "But the Sun's core is anything but ordinary. It's a huge nuclear reactor that converts matter into energy. In fact, it turns nearly five million tons of matter into energy every *second*."

Sean looked down at the plastic spoon in his hand. "You mean the energy I used to fling that marshmallow came from the center of the Sun? I'm doing the work of the cosmos! But it's kind of pathetic that that energy came all the way to Earth just to toss a marshmallow a few feet. That's gotta be a letdown."

"But energy can't be destroyed, either," Alberta

said. "So its time on Earth is just beginning." She leaned over her desk and peered down at the mini marshmallow. "But where did the energy go, exactly?"

Mr. Flask smiled and pressed a key on the keyboard. The videotape started moving again. The class watched as the marshmallow sailed horizontally through the air, rebounded off the wall, bounced along the floor a few times, and rolled to a stop.

"Who can trace the conversion of energy we just saw?" Mr. Flask asked.

Prescott raised his hand. "Well, first it bounced off the wall, which was a lot like my ball bouncing off the ground that time. So I guess the kinetic energy switched to potential energy, then back to kinetic energy again during the time the marshmallow changed direction."

Luis nodded. "So then the remaining kinetic energy carried the marshmallow back a few feet. Did it hit the floor because gravity was pulling on it?"

Mr. Flask nodded.

"It bounced a couple more times," Luis went on. "Then it rolled. And that's when it seemed to lose energy fast. But why?"

"It might be easier to understand with a slightly different example," Mr. Flask said. "Suppose Sean had launched a shape that couldn't roll, like a cube. Max, can you tell us what would happen if a cube hit the floor?"

Max Hoof frowned. "Well, it might bounce a little. Then it would slide along the floor until it stopped."

"What would make it stop?"

Max thought for a moment. "Maybe friction? I remember that the more you cut friction, the farther you can slide without stopping. That's why sleds are smooth on the bottom, right?"

Mr. Flask smiled. "Good point. Yes, friction removes energy from sliding objects. When all of the kinetic energy is gone from an object, it stops. Friction also removes energy from rolling objects, but not as quickly. Now, we know that energy can't be destroyed. So where did it go?"

Max looked down and shrugged. "I don't know, the ground?"

Mr. Flask nodded. "Can anyone tell me how?"

The class was silent.

"Friction is rubbing," Mr. Flask said. He held his hands palm to palm. "Rub your hands together, and see if you can figure out what friction does to mechanical energy. Here's a hint: You'll be able to *feel* it."

The classroom was filled with the *shooshing* sound of rubbed hands.

"Heat!" Luis blurted out. "My hands are getting warm. Is heat a kind of energy?"

The teacher smiled and nodded. "The heat from the rolling marshmallow warms up the ground."

Sean made a face. "You mean that if I roll a marshmallow across the floor, the ground underneath it will get hot?"

"Not hot," Mr. Flask said. "Just a tiny bit warmer. Interestingly, when your marshmallow was rolling across the floor, it was rubbing against something else, too. What was it?"

Alberta bit her lip. "Can we see the videotape again?"

"It wouldn't show up on the videotape."

Prescott glanced back at the professor. "Something that doesn't show up on videotape?" he asked nervously.

"You can't see it here in the classroom, either." Mr. Flask paused for a moment. "But it's all around you."

"Oh, *air*," Alberta said. "So if the marshmallow rubbed against the air, did the friction heat the air a little, too?"

"Great deduction!" Mr. Flask said. He reached into a desk drawer and pulled out a box of plastic spoons and a bag of mini marshmallows. He handed them to Prescott and Luis. "Pass these around, please." He turned to the class and smiled. "I'd like you to use this highly scientific equipment to explore kinetic and potential energy. Try to determine whether adding more potential energy to the spoon — that is, pulling the spoon back farther — causes there to be more kinetic energy in the marshmallow, which would send the marshmallow flying farther."

Prescott got to the back of the class and looked at the von Offels uncertainly. Would they want to try the experiment, too? He held out a spoon to Éduard.

Éduard frowned for a moment. Then he looked from side to side and reached for the spoon. "It's ridiculous, but why not?" he muttered.

The professor took a spoon without comment.

Esmerelda smiled but asked, "You wouldn't have anything bigger, dear?"

Prescott shook his head.

A few minutes later, it looked like a snowstorm was raging inside the science lab.

CHAPTER 4

Catapult!

Mr. Flask beamed as the occasional mini marshmallow bounced harmlessly off his head. He held up a bag of regular marshmallows. "When you're done testing changes in potential energy, come see how a change in marshmallow size affects your results."

Alberta was considering her loaded spoon. "Mr. Flask, how do I know for sure how much extra potential energy I'm putting in? It's hard to keep track of how much I'm bending the spoon."

"Great point, Alberta," Mr. Flask said. "This experiment definitely lacks precision. How would you change that?"

Alberta thought for a moment. "I guess I'd have to have a little gauge that showed me how far back I was pulling my spoon. Maybe it would be easier if it were mounted on my desk somehow."

Luis smiled. "A catapult!" He launched a large marshmallow across the room.

"That's a great idea," Sean said. "But not with this

wimpy little plastic spoon. How about we use one of those big serving spoons from the cafeteria?"

"Certainly not!" shouted a gruff voice from the hallway. Mr. Klumpp rushed in and immediately caught a marshmallow right between the eyes. "This is an outrage! The very sort of thing that —" He saw Aunt Esmerelda and stopped. She was trying to fling her mini marshmallow straight up into the air. "I, uh, hope you haven't given our visitors a bad impression of our school."

Luis turned to Alberta. "After that lunch," he whispered, "how could their impression get any worse?"

Aunt Esmerelda smiled at Mr. Klumpp. "Oh, we're having a lovely time. It seems Mr. Flask agrees with you and me: Sometimes it's glorious to take things to extremes."

Mr. Klumpp's mouth opened, but no sound came out.

"I can certainly promise that we'll take cleanup to extremes," Mr. Flask said. "The kids did a good job cleaning the cafeteria, didn't they?"

The custodian nodded mutely.

Aunt Esmerelda walked over and pressed her spoon and marshmallow into Mr. Klumpp's hand. "Try it for yourself."

He looked down, horror in his eyes. "I — I simply can't." He thrust them back at her and fled into the hallway.

"So, can we build that catapult?" Sean asked.

"Funny you should mention that," Mr. Flask said. "As you know, I live in the same house as many of my scientist ancestors did. They left behind a lot of interesting stuff. So believe it or not, I actually *have* a large catapult in my basement."

Professor von Offel's eyes opened wide.

"I told you Jedidiah stole that catapult," Atom whispered.

Von Offel shook his head in disbelief. "I didn't think he had it in him!"

"Well, you hardly gave him a choice," Atom replied. "He was under attack twenty-four hours a day."

"I was just certain one of the von Offel children misplaced it while ransacking the neighborhood," the professor said.

Alberta raised her hand. "How old is your catapult?"

"I don't know," Mr. Flask said. "I've looked through all of my ancestor Jedidiah's notebooks, but there's nothing in them about building a catapult. So it must have been one of his descendants' projects. Someday I need to comb through our family notes and see what I can find out about it."

"We could help," Luis offered.

Mr. Flask laughed. "Thanks, but you don't know how big a job it is. Jedidiah Flask had about 15 scientist descendants, and each one filled dozens of notebooks. I don't even have most of them. My father gave those notebooks to the research library at

Arcana Community College. They're locked away in the library's upper rooms, and even I need special permission to get to them."

"Who cares how old the catapult is?" Sean said. "All I want to know is, does it work?"

Luis rolled his eyes. "How would he know that, Sean? Do you think he's been launching it in his basement?"

"Actually, I did launch it once," the teacher said. "Remember the time I accidentally locked myself in the basement during the championship soccer match?"

The lab assistants swung around and looked at the professor, who stared back blankly.

"The basement is pretty deep, and all of the windows are up near the ceiling," Mr. Flask continued. "I paced around the basement for about an hour, trying to brainstorm a way out. I found a rope and spotted a high metal pipe near a window. But hard as I tried, I couldn't manage to throw the rope up over the pipe. Finally, I poked around a little more and uncovered the catapult. I tied an anchor to one end of the rope, loaded the anchor onto the catapult, and a few minutes later I was climbing to freedom."

"That's amazing!" Alberta said.

"You mean if you hadn't had the catapult, you wouldn't have made it to our match?" Prescott shuddered.

Sean frowned. "So the point of your story is that you haven't tested to see how far it can throw."

Mr. Flask laughed. "I guess you could look at it that way."

"Well, that's definitely something we can help with." Sean pointed toward the window. "Look at that big, empty school yard just waiting for someone to hurl large objects across it."

"That *would* be pretty cool," Luis said.

The teacher thought for a moment. "I'd have to ask Dr. Kepler first, of course. And I'm not completely sure whether I can even get the catapult out of the basement. But I'll try."

Sean pumped both of his fists into the air. "Yes!"

After school, the lab assistants headed for Alberta's house.

"I can't believe Dr. Kepler invited two new ghosts into our classroom," Prescott said. "Can't she tell there's something weird about them? I mean, look at the way they dress."

"I overheard her tell someone that the Third Millennium Foundation is headed by an eccentric billionaire," Alberta said. "She seems to think that's explanation enough. She also called the Millennium Foundation office and found out that Professor von Offel is supposed to turn in his report about Mr. Flask this Friday."

"Do you think his report will be positive?" Prescott asked.

Luis made a face. "The question is, will he turn in any report at all?"

Alberta stopped in her tracks. "But he *has* to," she said. "That's the whole reason he was sent here! If he doesn't — well, he'll be fired or something, right?"

Luis laughed. "This is a man who climbed a metal tower during a lightning storm. Do you really think he'd worry about losing a job?"

"Well, we can't just wait and see whether he turns in the report," Prescott said. "We have to take matters into our own hands."

CHAPTER 5

At Home
with the von Offels

The professor angrily paced the length of his parlor.

Atom watched from his perch. "But I *like* having Esmerelda and Éduard around again," he said. "Well, Esmerelda anyway. If Éduard had his way, I'd have to forage for food out in the yard. He thinks bird seed is too 'newfangled.' And he certainly doesn't like my sitting at the table."

The professor swung around again. "This house just isn't big enough for all of us," he insisted.

"What do you mean?" the parrot asked. "It's a mansion, for crying out loud."

"There's only one thing to do," von Offel said. "I've got to find a way to fix the deanimator. Then I can send them back where they belong and give myself what they have — 75 percent corporeality."

"You're jealous!" Atom said. "That's what this is really about, isn't it?"

The professor crossed his arms. "*I'm* the one who realized how perfect being 75 percent alive would be," he said. "But they're the ones reaping the benefits."

"But you were 65 percent alive before," Atom said. "Wasn't that close enough?"

"That extra 10 percent corporeality makes all the difference," von Offel insisted. "They can still walk through walls. But they can also see themselves in the mirror. They don't have to eat. But when they do, they can taste the food. They don't feel the lumps in the mattress. But they also don't sink into the bedsprings while they're sleeping."

Atom shrugged. "Okay, that part sounds like a worthy goal. So where do we begin?"

The professor dropped into a threadbare armchair. "That's just the problem," he moaned. "I have no idea. And young Flask has been absolutely no help. Where is Jedidiah Flask when you need him?" His eyes popped open, and he sat up excitedly. "That's it!"

Atom gulped. "You're not going to reanimate him, too, are you?"

"Only as a last resort," von Offel said. "First, I'm going to seek the help of some of his descendants."

Atom raised a feathered eyebrow. "But I thought Ethan was the only Flask left."

"Oh, I don't need a *live* Flask," the professor explained.

"This is what I was afraid of," Atom said.

"I just need those 15 dead Flasks that young Flask spoke about," von Offel continued. "More specifically, I need their notebooks. Within their pages lies a century of Flask thinking I never got to loot!"

Atom nodded. "And aren't likely to now, either. After all, those notebooks are locked in the upper storage rooms of the Arcana Community College library."

"That is a problem." The professor bared his teeth in a smile. "A problem that can be easily solved with a siege weapon. Luckily, I know just where to get one."

"Flask's catapult?" Atom asked. "But how will that help?"

"I'll send you ahead to open a library window," von Offel explained. "Then all I have to do is launch myself into the building."

Atom slapped his wing to his feathery forehead. "Do I really have to explain what a bad idea that is?"

The professor laughed.

"Oh, you were joking!" Atom said. "Whew!"

"I most certainly was not," the professor said. "I was merely enjoying the sight outside our picture window."

Atom spun around to watch. Outside, Mr. Flask and Aunt Esmerelda were on the steps of the Flask mansion. Mr. Flask was clearly trying to retreat inside.

Professor von Offel chuckled. "There's nothing more refreshing than watching a Flask squirm."

"It *is* a guilty pleasure," Atom said. "Uh-oh. Here comes trouble."

Éduard was marching across Mr. Flask's yard at a

furious pace. He grabbed Aunt Esmerelda by the arm and tugged her toward the von Offel mansion.

"I was only being neighborly!" Aunt Esmerelda insisted as they entered the front door.

"That was hardly a proper social call," Éduard said. "Standing on the man's front step."

"Things are a lot less formal in the 21st century," Aunt Esmerelda said. "You're going to have to get used to it."

"I have no intention of getting used to it," Éduard said. "I'm returning to where I belong as soon as it's possible."

"Here, here!" Professor von Offel clapped his hands. "Well said."

Aunt Esmerelda lifted an eyebrow. "And I suppose *you* intend to return to the grave with him?"

"Of course not," the professor said. "But don't let me stop you."

"*I'm* not going back to the grave, either," Aunt Esmerelda said. "I happen to like this new era. It's full of very big thinkers."

An hour later, the fight had blown over. Aunt Esmerelda was ladling the last stew out of an enormous pot.

Atom hopped up to his tiny bowl and took a sip. "This really is delicious, even if it's the tenth time we've had it."

"And what would you like for the next 10 days?" Aunt Esmerelda asked brightly.

Éduard peered into the huge cooking pot. "Couldn't you make a smaller batch next time?"

Aunt Esmerelda smiled regretfully. "You know I can only work big."

Éduard took a bite. "Well, it's delicious, if a little chewy at this date."

Aunt Esmerelda untied her apron and sat down to eat. "Over the next few days, I'm going to dedicate myself to making some more repairs around here."

Éduard glanced around nervously. "What repairs did you have in mind?"

Aunt Esmerelda shrugged. "I'm just going to take a look around and fix what's broken. Why?"

"Oh, nothing," Éduard said.

His aunt looked hurt. "Something's bothering you. Can't you tell me what it is?"

Éduard was silent.

The professor threw down his napkin. "What do you think it is? Even *I'm* alarmed by your habit of thinking big! Who knows what you'll do next? The new drapes you sewed are three yards too long. You built a *bonfire* in the fireplace. And you scrubbed a hole all the way through the kitchen floor."

Atom glanced anxiously at Aunt Esmerelda. Her face was twitching in a desperate attempt to maintain her composure. Finally, she broke down and laughed hysterically.

"Oh, all right!" she choked out. "I'll try to think a little smaller."

Bong! Bong!

Aunt Esmerelda stood up. "Is that the doorbell? Our first visitor! I hope it's that charming young teacher."

She opened the door. Alberta, Luis, and Prescott stood on the front porch.

"Oh, students from Ethan Flask's class!" Aunt Esmerelda stepped to one side. "Do come in."

The lab assistants didn't budge.

Alberta cleared her throat. "Um, could you please ask the professor to come to the door?"

"Is there some reason you don't want to come in?" Aunt Esmerelda asked.

"We had, well, kind of a scare last time we were here," Luis said.

"Yeah," Prescott muttered. "We were almost shoveled to death."

Aunt Esmerelda disappeared down the hallway.

Five full minutes later, the professor appeared at the door, with Atom on his shoulder. "Yes?"

"We're here about the Vanguard Teacher Award," Alberta began.

"The wha — oh, yes," the professor said. His face brightened. "You're not here to bribe me, by any chance?"

"Of course not!" Luis said.

"I knew that," the professor said.

"We just want to remind you that your deadline is tomorrow." Prescott held out a piece of paper. "We even, um, *dropped by* your office and dug out the evaluation form for you."

The professor stared at him blankly.

"You *do* plan to write the report on Mr. Flask, don't you?" Alberta asked.

"Awk! You write it! You write it!" Atom squawked.

The professor turned to face Atom. "These three busybodies know you can talk. If you have something to say, out with it!"

Atom sighed. "What I meant was, have them write it!" he said. "After all, who's in a better position to evaluate Flask than his own students? And you have so many other things on your mind."

"Why, that couldn't be any more brilliant if I'd thought of it myself!" von Offel said. He grabbed the evaluation form and disappeared into the mansion with it. A few minutes later, he returned and thrust it at Prescott.

There were two hastily scratched sentences at the top of the form. Prescott squinted and read aloud, "'Who's in a better position to evaluate Flask than his own students?'"

"Now, *that's* original," Atom said.

"'So that's what I've asked them to do,'" Prescott finished reading.

"Well, now," the professor said cheerfully. "The fate of your precious teacher is in your hands. I suggest you get right to work." He stepped inside and closed the door with a resounding *thud*.

CHAPTER 6

Power Play

When Prescott and Luis walked into science lab the next day, Alberta was sitting with her head on her desk.

Luis dropped into his chair and leaned toward her. "Are you okay?"

Alberta wearily pushed herself into an upright position. "Just tired, that's all. I stayed up kind of late working on Mr. Flask's recommendation. It doesn't have to be postmarked until tomorrow, but I wanted to make sure you guys got a chance to make any changes. Here, take a look."

Prescott and Luis huddled together to read the report.

"Perfect!" Prescott said several minutes later.

"Yeah. If the Foundation doesn't give Mr. Flask the award, I'll be amazed," Luis added

Alberta smiled. "Thanks."

"Should we drop it at the post office after school?" Luis asked.

"Sure," Alberta said. She rubbed her eyes. "All we

need is the professor's signature at the bottom, and we're golden."

Aunt Esmerelda entered the lab on Éduard's arm. She waved at the lab assistants as she swept by.

Prescott frowned. "Where's the professor? Shouldn't he be with them?"

"Well, he *has* been a little late each day since he became fully corporeal," Alberta said.

The bell rang. The whole class looked expectantly at the door. Mr. Flask glanced at his watch, then back at the door. Suddenly, there were footsteps at the door, and — Sean walked in.

He grinned at the teacher. "Sorry."

"Did you see the professor out in the hall?" the teacher asked him.

"Nope," Sean said. "Didn't see him at lunch, either, which was a shame, since he's the only one who can stand Mr. Klumpp's cooking."

"Actually, it wasn't that awful today," Max blurted out. He blushed. "I mean, well, actually it tasted pretty good."

Mr. Flask glanced at Aunt Esmerelda, who beamed at him. "I think Mr. Klumpp had a little help today," he said.

Alberta raised her hand. "Should I go check the professor's office?"

"No, that's okay." Mr. Flask looked back at Éduard and his aunt. "Do either of you know where the professor is?"

Éduard scowled. "I hate to even think."

Mr. Flask's eyebrows shot up.

"I'm sure he'd want you to carry on without him," Aunt Esmerelda said in a reassuring voice.

"Of course," the teacher said. He glanced back at Éduard, then at the door again. Finally, he faced the class. "Okay, today we're going to be experimenting with a more practical side of energy. For centuries, people have harnessed the energy of wind and put it to work. Today you're going to join them. Everybody form groups, three people per."

He handed Alberta a box of drinking straws. "One straw per group, including our guests, of course. Luis, two of these paper plates per group. And Prescott, check that box over there, and give each group a drinking glass. Now, let's see, everyone needs some tape and scissors."

Max raised his hand. "Could I pass those out?"

"Sure, Max." Mr. Flask held up a paper plate and began demonstrating how to cut and fold the windmill blade.

"Wind power is something I heartily approve of," Éduard announced as the class worked. "Relying on an energy source as erratic and uncontrollable as the wind — it takes a strong resolve to stand up to the inevitable windless days or even weeks. Then there are the frequent mechanical breakdowns." He sniffed importantly. "Builds character."

Mr. Flask suppressed a smile. "Luckily, those with

a less rugged spirit can build their windmills in places with more predictable, steady winds."

"As if," Sean said. "Who needs energy from the wind when you can just plug your TV into the wall?"

"You don't think electricity magically appears in your outlets, do you?" Alberta said. "It had to come from some kind of power plant."

"Good point," Mr. Flask said. "Just over half of our nation's electrical power is generated by burning coal. Nearly a fifth comes from nuclear energy. The other major sources are natural gas, hydropower, and oil."

Prescott raised his hand. "What's hydropower?"

"Water power," the teacher explained. "Which we'll experiment with tomorrow."

Luis was attaching his group's windmill blade to the inside of a drinking glass. "So, why wasn't wind power on that list?" he asked.

"It's a small but growing source of electricity," Mr. Flask said.

Sean frowned. "What? People are actually building new windmills? Are they wearing those clunky wooden shoes, too?"

Mr. Flask laughed. "The new windmills, called turbines, are very high-tech. Each one looks like an enormous propeller hoisted high in the air on a metal pole. As a turbine's blades spin in the wind, they activate a generator, which produces electricity.

In some places with strong, steady winds, there are entire 'wind farms' with acres of turbines. Other times a home has only one turbine. There are even a few schools that have them."

Prescott looked around the room. "But what happens if the wind stops?" he asked. "Do the lights just go out?"

"Yeah, does everyone get to go home?" Sean added.

"The wind-powered schools I've read about are also connected to regular power lines," Mr. Flask said. "While the turbine turns, the school gets electricity from wind power. Then, when the wind stops, it gets electricity from the power company instead. And if the turbine makes more electricity than the school needs, the power company buys at least some of the surplus."

"Do you think Dr. Kepler would let *our* school get a turbine?" Luis asked.

"I'm sure she'd love it — *if* it made any sense for us," the teacher said. "Unfortunately, our school property just isn't windy enough. The wind-powered schools I mentioned are in Iowa. It must be a lot windier out there. Actually, the state with the most wind energy potential is North Dakota. Scientists calculate that under perfect conditions, North Dakota could supply one third of all the electricity for the nation."

"That would mean we'd burn a lot less coal," Alberta said. "And *that* would mean a lot less pollution. Also, we wouldn't have to worry so much about running out of oil or natural gas."

Mr. Flask nodded. "Wind power is a *renewable* energy source. That means it can't run out. Hydropower is also renewable, as is solar power, energy from the Sun."

"I almost forgot about solar power," Alberta said. "How come it wasn't on your list of energy sources?"

"Well, like wind power, it only produces a tiny amount of our nation's electricity," Mr. Flask said.

"But it's a perfect energy solution!" Alberta said. "Like wind, sunlight is free and doesn't pollute."

"I'm a huge fan of solar energy," Mr. Flask said. "I even have some photovoltaic cells on top of my house. But it's not a perfect energy solution yet. So far, the technology is really too expensive for most people. Scientists are working on making it cheaper. But in the meantime, it could take my system 12 years to pay for itself."

"What do you mean?" Alberta said.

"Well, say it cost me $24,000 to buy and install my panels. Then each year, suppose they generate enough electricity to save me $2,000 on my energy bill. It would take 12 years for those savings to add up to my original investment."

"Twelve years is forever!" Max said. "We'll be in college by then!"

"But *after* 12 years, your panels will keep on making free electricity, right?" Luis asked.

"Exactly," Mr. Flask said. "And as Alberta pointed out, it will also be pollution-free electricity. The technology is so new that no one knows how long the solar panels will last. They could keep generating free electricity for 50 more years, or even longer."

"So the payoff is huge," Luis said. "It's just that $24,000 is a lot of money to scrape together."

The teacher nodded. "Like I said, I'm sure the technology will get cheaper and better. Hey, maybe one of you will grow up to invent solar cells that everyone can afford."

Alberta raised her hand. "Our schoolyard doesn't get much wind, but it does get a lot of sun," she said. "Do you think Dr. Kepler would let us have photovoltaic cells if we could raise the money somehow?"

Mr. Flask thought for a moment. "Actually, there *are* programs that help schools purchase and install solar equipment. Solar panels can be a good science experiment as well as a clean energy source. Tomorrow, if we finish our waterwheels early, we can do a computer search for more information."

Alberta smiled and turned to Luis and Prescott. "He just gets cooler all the time," she whispered. "Maybe I should add another paragraph to the recommendation."

Prescott glanced back at the professor's empty desk. "There's only one thing we need to add to that form — Professor von Offel's signature. Why isn't he here today?"

"Don't sweat it," Luis whispered. "He's probably out sick or something. If he's not in tomorrow, we'll stop by the von Offel mansion after school."

CHAPTER 7

Once Dead, Always Dead?

That evening, Aunt Esmerelda pushed an enormous pot of soup to the table on a large cart. "Have seconds, everyone," she said. "There's plenty."

The professor dug into his soup immediately.

Esmerelda smiled. "Looks like you worked up a real appetite today," she said.

The professor wiped his forehead on his dirt-soiled shirtsleeve and grunted.

Éduard frowned as Atom hopped eagerly over to his little bowl. "Doesn't this century have any kind of social norms regarding the place of pets?"

"But Atom isn't a pet, dear," Esmerelda said as she ladled up some soup for the parrot. "He's a long-standing member of the von Offel family."

"That's nonsense," Éduard said. "All of the von Offels I remember were distinctly human."

"Then I suppose you didn't hear about your grandson, Colin von Offel, transplanting his brain into the body of a wildebeest," Esmerelda said.

"Atom tells me they got musky-smelling postcards from Africa for years afterward."

"Well, that's certainly improper, too — if Atom is to be believed, of course," Éduard said.

Atom rolled his eyes and took another sip of soup.

Éduard sniffed. "But I still think the proper place for his bowl is on the floor."

Aunt Esmerelda banged the ladle onto the table and put her hands on her hips. "I'm sorry, Éduard. But considering you think that the proper place for the *humans* at this table is the von Offel crypt, I'm not inclined to bow to your wishes. Atom has done everything he could to make our reentry into this world as pleasant as possible. I should think you'd be grateful. But perhaps I'm being unrealistic, since you can't even be grateful for our second chance at life!" She dropped into her chair and picked up her spoon. "I'm sorry to blow up so," she muttered. "But you know I only do things big."

After an awkward moment, Éduard cleared his throat. "I apologize, Aunt Esmerelda, but —"

"Your apology should go to Atom!" she said.

Éduard made a face. "All right then, Atom. I apologize for suggesting that you eat on the floor."

Atom held out his bowl for seconds. "Don't mention it. Already forgotten."

"Perhaps you would be more comfortable in a *cage*," Éduard continued.

The professor paused between bites. "You're playing with fire, man," he said.

"Well, anyway," Éduard said, "I've changed my mind. I no longer believe we should return to the grave."

The professor froze in midbite. "What? You're turning your back on your principles? Wasn't it only two days ago you were telling me that the supreme law of the universe is 'Once dead, always dead'?"

"Yes," Éduard said. "But that was before I sat in on Ethan Flask's sixth-grade science class."

The professor slapped his forehead. "It would be just like young Flask to make life sound worth living, blast him!"

"Not *living*, exactly," Éduard said. "But he did make life sound worth *haunting*."

Aunt Esmerelda brightened a little. "That sounds interesting. Tell us about it."

"Well, haunting is a proud tradition that goes back centuries at least," Éduard explained. "And who better for the job than a dead person like myself?"

"Good point," Aunt Esmerelda said. "That would be very proper."

"The duties are light: some moaning here, some creaking floorboards there," Éduard continued. "Maybe some rattling of chains when there are guests present."

Aunt Esmerelda nodded. "One should always go out of one's way for visitors."

The professor's eyes narrowed. "And exactly

where were you planning to haunt? Not the von Offel mansion, I hope."

"Oh, no," Éduard said. "You could see right
through me, figuratively speaking, of course."

"What about Ethan Flask's house?" Aunt Esmerelda suggested. "You're interested in his work,
and you'd be close enough to visit us often."

"I had the same idea," Éduard said. "So today,
right after school, I gave myself a tour of the Flask
mansion."

"Well, *that* certainly doesn't sound very proper,"
Aunt Esmerelda scolded him.

Éduard reddened a little. "Well, how do you think
most ghosts approach a house? Ring the bell and ad-
vertise their services? At any rate, it's a moot point,
because I could never haunt there."

"Why not?" Aunt Esmerelda asked.

Éduard glanced at Atom. "Residing with a parrot
is one thing —"

"That's 'The World's Only Genius Parrot' to you,
buddy," Atom said.

"But Ethan Flask has a veritable zoo over there,"
Éduard continued. "There are animals in and
around his house. Many of them grunt, squeak,
chirp, cheep, hoot, snarl, or yap. Ghosts don't need
sleep, but surely we deserve some peace and quiet
every once in a while."

"My sentiments exactly," the professor said.

"On top of that," Éduard continued, "the current

Flask's housekeeping leaves something to be desired. You wouldn't believe what a mess his basement is. It looks like someone ransacked it! He leaves the door wide open, and the lock is even broken. I really expected Ethan Flask to pay a little more attention to detail."

Aunt Esmerelda looked at the professor curiously. "Where did you say you were today, Grandfather?"

"I *didn't* say," he told her flatly.

She considered him for another moment, then turned back to Éduard. "So if you can't haunt the von Offel or Flask mansions, where can you haunt?" she asked him. "Surely not the school."

"No, ghosts do their best work at night, so it has to be a home," Éduard said. "I'll simply have to give the matter some more thought."

The professor pushed himself away from the table. "Well, feel free to think fast and get out soon."

Éduard threw up his hands. "But I can't go out haunting like this!" he said. "Everyone can see me plain as day. I still need you to fix that deanimator. But instead of deanimating me completely, I just want you to adjust me — about 20 percent corporeality should be right for the job."

"What?" the professor said. "But you're 75 percent corporeal now. What could be more perfect?"

"For haunting, 20 percent," Éduard insisted.

The professor looked at Aunt Esmerelda, who shrugged.

"Actually, I'd like to be *more* corporeal myself," she said. "I want to live my new life to the fullest."

Professor von Offel stood up and looked at his two descendants. "I've never heard anything so ridiculous in my life — or in my death, either," he said. "I'm just glad my father will never know how quickly the von Offel line went downhill after me." He stormed out of the room.

Atom was scraping the bottom of his third bowl of soup. He rocked back on his tail and gave a contented burp. "I suppose I ought to fly after him," he said lazily. "Maybe after just one more bowl."

CHAPTER 8

Down to the Wire

The next afternoon, the lab assistants rushed to get to science class a little early. Mr. Flask was unloading a box of Styrofoam disks.

"Professor von Offel wasn't at lunch again today," Prescott said to the teacher. "Have you heard from him?"

Mr. Flask shook his head. "I'm guessing he took off yesterday and today to write his report for the Millennium Foundation. You probably didn't know this, but it has to be in the mail by five P.M. today."

The lab assistants shared a look.

Mr. Flask glanced back at the professor's empty desk. "I should have realized he'd stop attending our class sometime this week. But he's been here for so long, it's hard to imagine life at Einstein Elementary without him. It'll certainly be a lot less eventful."

Luis rolled his eyes. "I guess that's one way to put it," he muttered.

"I wouldn't worry," Mr. Flask went on. "I'm sure

he'll stop by at some point, maybe next week. He couldn't spend all that time with us and then disappear without saying good-bye."

A moment later, Éduard and Aunt Esmerelda arrived. The lab assistants met them at the door.

"We've *got* to see Professor von Offel," Luis told them. "Do you know where he is?"

"I'm afraid not," Éduard said as he passed by. "He's in a bit of a snit. Won't say a word to me."

Aunt Esmerelda paused. "Why don't you come by the house this evening?" she suggested. "He never misses supper. You can see him then." She smiled kindly and glided away.

"Thanks," Luis called after her. Then he lowered his voice. "Of course, by then it will be too late."

"No, by then we will have already found him," Prescott said firmly.

Alberta nodded. "Let's meet on the sidewalk as soon as school ends. We'll look everywhere."

"Count me in," Luis said.

The bell rang. Mr. Flask motioned for the lab assistants to come forward. "Alberta, could you give each lab group three paper plates? Prescott, please hand out one pencil per group. Luis, they also need paper clips. And let's see, uh, *Max*, could you give each group a roll of masking tape?"

Max beamed as he passed Prescott. "Maybe I'll make lab assistant after all," he said. Prescott smiled back.

"Remember those windmills we made yesterday?" asked Mr. Flask. "Today I challenge you all to turn these materials into waterwheels."

Half an hour later, each group was testing its waterwheel over a plastic tub.

"Pretty cool," Max said. "Ours works almost exactly like a real waterwheel."

Sean laughed. "What are you, a waterwheel expert?"

"Just about." Max smiled. "Remember, my mom is president of the Daughters of Arcana. She's dragged me to tons of historic sites. And it seems like half of them have waterwheels."

Heather raised her hand. "My family visited Hoover Dam last summer. It uses water to make electricity, but it didn't look a thing like this experiment."

Mr. Flask nodded. "Hydropower has changed a lot since people used wooden wheels to run a town's grain mill. These days, most hydropower is generated by turbines at the bottom of giant dams."

Alberta raised her hand. "Are those turbines like the wind turbines we studied yesterday?"

"Well, water turbines look different," Mr. Flask said. "But the basic principle is the same. It's just water moving them instead of wind."

"So why put water turbines at the bottom of a dam?" Prescott asked.

"A dam holds back running water, creating what's basically a tall stack of water on the upstream side," the teacher explained. "That stack allows the water to produce more electricity. Let me show you."

Mr. Flask reached into a box on his desk and pulled out a plastic cup and a plastic bowl. He carried them to the sink and filled the bowl with water. He poured the water into the cup. Then he filled the bowl again. "You just saw me put equal amounts of water into this bowl and this cup," he said. "Heather, could you come up and tell me any differences you observe between the two?"

Heather walked over and peered into the cup, then the bowl. "Well, the water in the bowl is more spread out and not as deep. I guess the water in the cup is more like the stack you were talking about."

The teacher nodded. "Now, before class, I made a hole in the side of each of these. Both holes are the same size and the same distance from the base."

"Then how come there's no water pouring out?" Sean asked.

Mr. Flask smiled. "My thumbs are covering both holes. But in a moment I'm going to move my thumbs and hold the cup and bowl over the sink. I want you to tell me what you observe. Ready? Go!"

Alberta watched a thin stream of water shoot out of each hole. "Hey, the stream from the cup shoots out farther," she said. "Does that mean it has more energy somehow?"

The teacher nodded. "The water at the bottom of the cup is under more pressure than the water at the bottom of the bowl. That's because the water at the bottom of the cup is under a taller stack of water. The higher pressure makes the cup's water shoot out faster and farther. In a hydroelectric plant, the higher pressure makes the water turn the turbines faster — which generates more electricity."

Mr. Flask looked at his watch. "Let's go ahead and start cleaning up now," he said. "Then I'll take some volunteers to start that solar energy computer search we talked about." He reached under the sink and grabbed a handful of sponges. "Oh, I forgot. I have some bad news. It's hard to believe, but yesterday during school, someone broke into my basement and took my catapult."

"Oh, *man!*" Sean said. "That stinks."

Luis sat up a little straighter. "Are you sure it was stolen during school?"

"I know it was there yesterday morning, because I went down and measured it." Mr. Flask laughed. "I'd asked Dr. Kepler whether I could bring it to school, and not surprisingly she wanted to know just how big a catapult we were talking about. So anyway, it was definitely there in the morning. And when I got home from school yesterday afternoon, the first thing I noticed was that the basement door was open. When I looked closer, I saw that the lock was broken. There was a huge mess, and the catapult was gone."

"What did the cops say?" Sean asked.

"Well, I haven't contacted them yet," Mr. Flask

said. "It seemed more like a prank than a crime, though I'm not sure Detective Shapiro would agree. I just can't imagine what anyone would want with a stolen catapult. It's not like you could use it without attracting a lot of attention."

Across town, Professor von Offel was struggling to pull a large wooden object down the sidewalk. Atom was pushing it from the rear, his wings flapping wildly. As pedestrians jumped aside to avoid the hulking mass, the professor scowled. "What are you staring at?" he snapped. "Haven't you ever seen a siege weapon before?"

CHAPTER 9

The Professor's Big Fling

Twenty minutes after school let out, the lab
assistants were standing on the porch of
the von Offel mansion. Luis took a deep
breath. "Here goes nothing," he said, and rang the
bell.

A moment later, Aunt Esmerelda opened the door.
"Hello, children," she said. "I'm sorry, but my
grandfather isn't home right now. I probably should
have been more specific about when we eat. I suppose dining hours must have changed considerably
since I was alive."

"Oh, no," Alberta said. "My family doesn't eat until 6:30. We know we're early. It's just that —"

"Are those the children from Ethan Flask's class?"
called a voice down the hallway. A moment later,
Éduard appeared next to his aunt. "I've been want-
ing to talk to you three. Can you tell me about the
Daughters of Arcana?"

"You want to join the Daughters of Arcana?" Luis
asked. "But I think most of the members are, well,
daughters."

"No, no, no," Éduard said. "I just wondered whether it was a historical society of some kind."

Prescott nodded. "Yeah, I think Max's mother started it. It's a group of women who get together to learn more about the history of Arcana."

"Are they interested in historic landmarks?" Éduard asked.

"Yes, very," Alberta said slowly. "Is this by any chance about the von Offel tower?"

"The wha — oh, my goodness, that overbuilt death trap?" Éduard pounded his fist into his hand. "I've always said that people weren't meant to build that high. Don't tell me it has remained standing all these years."

"No, it fell down, all right," Prescott said.

"Well, I hope the nation took a lesson from it," Éduard said. "And that no one ever tried to build that tall again."

Aunt Esmerelda studied Prescott's face shrewdly. "I have a feeling, Éduard, that humanity has built considerably higher."

Éduard frowned. "Well, anyway, all I really wanted to know was whether the Daughters of Arcana were interested in the town's historic homes."

"I think so," Prescott said. "I mean, Max's house is probably about as old as this one."

"Excellent," Éduard said. "And this Max is the other boy who was at the von Offel crypt, right?"

Prescott nodded.

"What is his surname?" Éduard asked.

"His 'sir name'?" Prescott said. "I didn't know he was a Sir. His mom must *love* that."

"No, dear," Aunt Esmerelda said. "Éduard wants to know the name he shares with the rest of his family, like we share 'von Offel.'"

"Oh, his *last* name," Prescott said. "It's Hoof. Max Hoof."

Éduard turned to his aunt. "Hoof. Hmm, I wonder whether he's descended from Smedley Hoof?"

Aunt Esmerelda raised her eyebrows. "Perhaps, but I think it would be most polite not to mention it. He seems like a nice boy."

"Do you suppose his family lives in the old Hoof mansion?" Éduard said. "I always thought it was a little showy, but —"

Alberta glanced at Luis, who nodded.

"Excuse me," Alberta interrupted. "But we're actually here about something pretty important. You know that the professor is supposed to be writing a report about Mr. Flask for the Millennium Foundation, right?'

Aunt Esmerelda looked puzzled. "But Atom said that *you* were going to write it."

"We did." Alberta held up the envelope. "But we need the professor's signature before we can send it. And it has to be in the mail today."

Luis looked at his watch. "In the next hour and 20 minutes."

"Goodness," Aunt Esmerelda said. "Okay, well,

let's see. The last time we saw him was when we were leaving for school today."

"What was he doing?" Luis asked.

"Sitting with his hands folded," Aunt Esmerelda said. "Which seemed a little fishy to me at the time."

"Did he say why he wasn't coming to school?" Prescott asked.

"Well, not today," Aunt Esmerelda replied. "But yesterday he announced that he was through with Ethan Flask, that he'd found other Flasks to help him."

"Help him do what?" Prescott asked.

Aunt Esmerelda thought for a moment. "Well, as you know, my grandfather hates being fully alive. He wants to fix his deanimator so that he can make his existence more bearable. But he doesn't have a clue how to do it."

"Of course, he'd never ask *us* for help," Éduard said, "even though we're his own flesh and blood."

"Well, grandfather stubbornly clings to the old von Offel ways," Aunt Esmerelda said. "He always insisted that we had a special relationship with the Flasks."

"I believe the word he used was 'parasitic,'" Éduard said.

Aunt Esmerelda nodded. "Anyway, initially he hoped Ethan Flask's class lectures would give him some ideas. But apparently he now has some other source." She trailed off.

"But where would he find other Flasks?" Alberta asked. "I thought Mr. Flask was the last one left in his family."

Prescott's eyes grew wide. "Do the Flasks have a family crypt?"

"I'm not sure," Aunt Esmerelda said. "But his deanimator, which, as you know, is also a reanimator, is still sitting in the living room. So I don't think he's out bringing dead Flask scientists back to life, if that's what you're afraid of."

Alberta thought for a moment. "Didn't Mr. Flask say something about a group of Flask scientists this week?"

Luis snapped his fingers. "The college library!" he said. "Remember, he said there were a bunch of his family's science journals in the library of the Arcana Community College."

"Do you think the professor might be trying to find an answer in one of those journals?" Alberta asked. "But it sounded as if there were hundreds of them."

Aunt Esmerelda smiled. "That does sound like a lot of work for Grandfather, but perhaps he's exhausted every other option."

"The community college is halfway across town," Prescott said. "We'd better get going."

"Would you like me to go with you?" Aunt Esmerelda asked.

"No, that's okay," Alberta replied. "But if the professor comes back home, could you try to keep him here? If we don't find him at the college, we'll be back."

Aunt Esmerelda nodded.

As the lab assistants left the von Offel property, Prescott pointed out Mr. Flask standing next to his basement door. The teacher was talking to a man with a notebook.

"Looks like Detective Shapiro," Alberta said.

Luis nodded. "I wonder whether we'll be bailing Mr. Flask out of jail tonight."

"Luis!" Alberta said

"Kidding, kidding," he said. "It's just hard to forget the way Detective Shapiro treated Mr. Flask that time stuff was disappearing around the school."

They walked for a few blocks in silence.

When they reached the campus, Prescott said, "I wonder who *did* steal the catapult."

Alberta nodded. "What I don't get is, how did they even know it was down there?"

Luis made a face. "I can't believe you guys. It had to have been the professor. Think about it. He was in school two days ago when Mr. Flask told us about the catapult. Then yesterday, when it was stolen, he was mysteriously absent."

"That *does* make sense," Prescott said.

"Except for one thing," Alberta said. "What would the professor want with a catapult?"

Luis shrugged. "I don't know. But I think we're

about to find out." He pointed down the walkway that ran along the side of the library. There, beyond the bushes, were the professor, Atom, and the catapult.

Alberta took off running, and Luis and Prescott followed. When they reached the catapult, the professor was climbing into the catapult's launching arm. Atom was perched next to the control lever.

"Professor von Offel," Alberta shouted, "please climb down."

"Not a chance!" the professor said. "Not when I'm so close to my ultimate goal!"

"Unless your ultimate goal is to be hurled against a brick wall and have severe internal bleeding, then please climb down," Luis said.

The professor frowned. "Atom opened a window for me." He pointed to the third story. "I'm going to launch myself through that window. Then I'll take possession of all the Flask secrets within."

"But how do you know the catapult is aimed right?" Alberta asked.

"Impeccable von Offel judgment," the professor said.

"Uh-oh," Atom muttered. "Suddenly I'm getting a bad feeling about this."

"But there's no room for error," Alberta shouted. "Remember, you're 100 percent corporeal now."

"Not after my work here is complete!" the professor proclaimed.

"Yeah," Luis said to Prescott. "He might be zero percent corporeal again."

"Ready. Set. Throw the lever!" the professor shouted.

Instead, Atom fluttered up and landed on his shoulder. "I'm having second thoughts about this," the parrot explained. "Maybe we should test the catapult first."

"Nonsense!" the professor said. "Young Flask said it worked. And we all know how fastidious those Flasks are."

"Well, I just can't help you hurl your life away, Johannes," Atom said. "Not after we've been through so much."

"Then fly away, you frightened fledgling," the professor snapped. "I've got work to do." He unzipped his shoe and hefted it in his hand. Then he took aim at the lever and threw.

The lever shifted suddenly. Atom squawked and launched himself straight up. The catapult arm sprang forward. First it caught Atom's tail feathers and sent him tumbling beak over claws. Then it pitched the professor's body toward the side of the library.

The lab assistants watched, frozen with horror.

Suddenly, the professor's body was lit by a beam of bright light. Less than a second later, he hit the wall a good yard from the window — and passed right through.

The lab assistants swung around. There was Aunt Esmerelda, with the professor's deanimator on her shoulder.

She smiled sheepishly. "I've been doing some home repairs the last few days, and after you left I decided to tackle this," she said. "It was surprisingly easy to fix, just a question of bad alignment, really. I adjusted Éduard to 20 percent corporeality. He was delighted and immediately floated off to see about haunting the Hoof mansion."

Alberta cringed. "He's going to give Max a heart attack! Or at least a double-nostril nosebleed."

"I don't know," Prescott said. "I think Max has gotten a little tougher in the past few weeks."

"After that success, I thought maybe I should bring the deanimator over here," Aunt Esmerelda continued. "Just in case it could be of some help."

"How did you get here so fast?" Luis asked.

"Well, first I adjusted myself to 33 percent corporeality. That helped me travel a lot lighter," Aunt Esmerelda said.

Alberta leaned forward. "Now that you mention it, I can see through you just a bit."

"Hey, look," Prescott said.

The professor was standing at the open window. He climbed out onto the ledge, then jumped three stories to the ground. He walked casually over to the group. "I told you my plan would work," he said.

"Boy, you sure did," Alberta said.

Luis made a face. "What?"

Prescott put a finger to his lips. "She only agreed that the professor *said* it would work," he whispered to Luis.

Alberta slid an envelope out of her backpack and unfolded the observation report on Mr. Flask. "Could we get your signature on this, professor?"

The professor patted his pockets. "I don't seem to have a quill on me."

"Here, use my ballpoint pen," Alberta said. She carefully clicked it open and held it out to him.

The professor quickly signed the paper. Alberta shoved it into the envelope. "Let's get this to the post office." She glanced over at the catapult. "Then maybe we should stop by Mr. Flask's house and tell him to call off the search."

The lab assistants waved at Aunt Esmerelda and took off.

Atom landed unsteadily on the professor's shoulder.

"Come crawling back, have you?" von Offel said.

"No," Atom gulped. "Flying."

The professor turned to his granddaughter. "Well, 75 percent corporeality is all I predicted it would be. I highly recommend you stick with it."

Aunt Esmerelda shook her head. "You know I can't do anything in a small way."

Atom's eyes grew wide. "Not 200 percent corporeality?"

She looked wistfully at the deanimator. "I don't

think that's possible," she said. "One hundred percent will have to suffice."

"What will you do now?" Atom asked.

"Naturally, I'd like to keep living at the von Offel mansion," she said.

Atom turned toward the professor. "Let her stay. I can't live without her soup."

The professor frowned.

"And not to put too fine a point on it, she just saved your life," Atom continued.

"Oh, all right," the professor replied.

Aunt Esmerelda smiled. "What I really want to do is get back into science, but it's clear I have some catching up to do first. In the meantime, Dr. Kepler has offered me the job of cafeteria cook. It plays to my strengths, of course, because I like to work big." She paused and colored slightly. "And being at the school will also give me a chance to get to know that darling man better."

Atom ducked his head in embarrassment. "I'm not sure how to say this," he began, "but I don't think Ethan Flask is the man for you."

Aunt Esmerelda laughed. "Oh, he was just a passing fancy. I meant George, of course. George Klumpp."

Welcome to the World of
MAD SCIENCE!

The Mad Science Group has been providing live, interactive, exciting science experiences for children throughout the world for more than 12 years. Our goal is to provide children with fun, entertaining, and exciting activities that instill a clearer understanding of what science is really about and how it affects the world around them. Founded in Montreal, Canada, we currently have 125 locations throughout the world.

Our commitment to science education is demonstrated throughout this imaginative series that mixes hilarious fiction with factual information to show how science plays an important role in our daily lives. To add to the learning fun, we've also created exciting, accessible experiment logs so that children can bring the excitement of hands-on science right into their homes.

To discover more about Mad Science and how to bring our interactive science experience to your home or school, check out our website:
http://www.madscience.org

We spark the imagination and curiosity
of children everywhere!